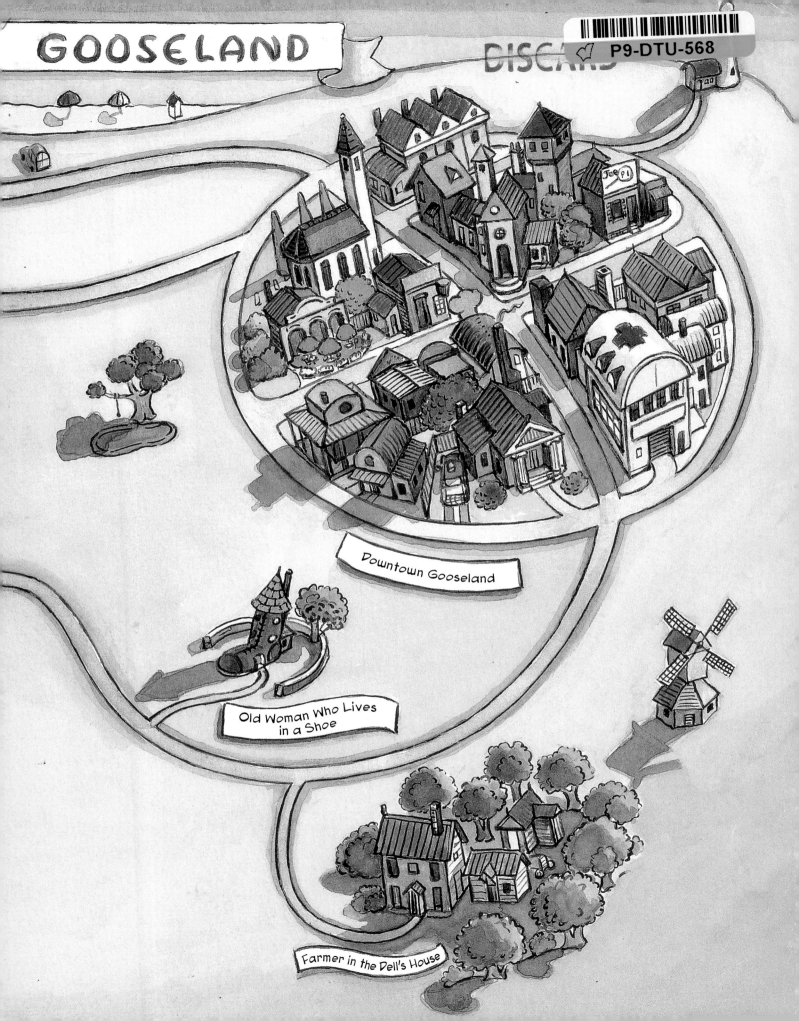

GOOSELAND

Downtown Gooseland

Old Woman Who Lives in a Shoe

Farmer in the Dell's House

What REALLY Happened to Humpty?

(from **the** files of a hard-boiled detective)

by
Joe Dumpty

as told to
Jeanie Franz Ransom

illustrated by
Stephen Axelsen

Charlesbridge

For my egg-cellent editor, Randi, and Aunt Kris
—J. F. R.

For Joey, a good egg
—S. A.

Published by Charlesbridge
85 Main Street
Watertown, MA 02472
(617) 926-0329
www.charlesbridge.com

Library of Congress Cataloging-in-Publication Data
Ransom, Jeanie Franz, 1957–
  What really happened to Humpty? : from the files of a hard-boiled detective /
as told to Jeanie Franz Ransom ; illustrated by Stephen Axelsen.
    p. cm.
  Summary: Detective Joe Dumpty rushes to investigate the mysterious
circumstances under which his older brother, Humpty, fell from a wall on
his first day as captain of the new Neighborhood Watch program.
  ISBN 978-1-58089-109-7 (reinforced for library use)
[1. Characters in literature—Fiction. 2. Mystery and detective stories.
3. Humorous stories.] I. Axelsen, Stephen, ill. II. Title.
PZ7.R1744Whd 2009
[E]—dc22   2008007232

Printed in China
(hc) 10 9 8 7 6 5 4 3 2 1

Illustrations done in watercolor and pen and ink on Canson Montval 300 gsm paper
Display type and text type set in Typeka Mix, American Typewriter, and Blambot Pro
Color separations by Chroma Graphics, Singapore
Printed and bound by Jade Productions
Production supervision by Brian G. Walker
Designed by Diane M. Earley

Humpty Dumpty sat on a wall.

Humpty Dumpty had a great fall.

Humpty Dumpty was pushed.

At least I think so. Who am I? I'm Joe Dumpty, Humpty's younger brother.

You probably haven't heard of me. I never was Mother's favorite. Mother Goose, that is. Ever since she became Police Chief Goose, she thinks I'm just stirring up trouble with my detective business.

Yes, Mother Goose always liked Humpty best. He's such a good egg. That's why I think it's a crime that he fell off the Wall. After all, he'd been sitting up there for as long as I can remember with no problems whatsoever. Until that awful, scrambled-up day.

It was a picture-book-perfect morning. The Old Woman Who Lives in a Shoe had just dropped off her kids at the Jack 'n' Jill Day Care Center. The Three Little Pigs were putting the finishing touches on their latest house. And across the field, Humpty was sitting on the Wall.

I wish I'd stopped to crack a few jokes with my brother—but it was Humpty's first week as captain of our new Neighborhood Watch program, and I didn't want to distract him.

Besides, it was almost nine, and I had to get to work.

I made a quick stop and ran into Little Red Riding Hood.

"The Muffin Man's scrambling to fill a big order,"

Red said. "I can't even buy one lousy muffin for my

grandmother!" She sniffed loudly and stomped off in a huff.

With my espresso in hand, I headed to the office.

As I opened my office door, the phone rang. It was Little
Miss Muffet. "Joe, something's happened to Humpty!"

I raced to the Wall. Miss Muffet was there, cell phone in hand. "I called 911," she sobbed.

I looked at my brother. He wasn't making a sound. Whoever did this was gonna fry!

I walked back around the Wall, and that's when I saw it.
Something shiny was tucked under Miss Muffet's tuffet.
She was on the phone, so I didn't bother asking if I could
look under her tuffet. I just did.

Sometimes detectives have to act first and ask questions later.

It was a pair of binoculars. Not just any binoculars. These puppies were the Official Binoculars of the Neighborhood Watch program. Humpty had been showing them off ever since he'd become captain.

Were you looking under my tuffet?

"What are you doing with those?" Muffy asked, grabbing the binoculars. I was just about to ask her the same thing, when . . .

. . . all the king's horses and all the king's men arrived. They couldn't put Humpty together again, so they scooped him up and rushed to the hospital.

"What's the story?" I asked Muffy. I wanted some answers.

Muffy sighed. "I was just shooting the breeze with Humpty, waiting for Spider. Humpty was letting me try his binoculars when suddenly this huffy-puffy wind blew him right off the Wall!"

Police Chief Goose pulled up in her big honking cruiser. "I was at the Three Pigs'," she apologized. "The wind we had this morning blew down their new house."

"I just told Joe that the wind made Humpty fall," Muffy said.

"*I* made Humpty fall," said a small voice out of nowhere.

"It's my fault," Spider said, dropping down from the tree. "I was rushing to get down here by nine this morning—my usual time—when this puff of wind pushed me straight toward Humpty. I must have scared him, because the next thing I knew, Humpty was on the ground. I zipped home, but I knew I had to 'fess up. Humpty was my friend."

"My brother wasn't afraid of anything! That's why he was the perfect Neighborhood Watch captain. What happened to Humpty wasn't your fault, Spider," I said.

"It wasn't anybody's fault," Muffy chimed in. "It was an accident."

"Agreed," Chief Goose said. "Go on to the hospital, Joe," she told me. "I'll write up an accident report."

"But Chief, Humpty's been sitting on the Wall for years
without a wobble," I said. "Then the first week he's
Neighborhood Watch captain, he suddenly falls off?
The same day the Pigs' house blows down? Coincidence?
I don't think so."

Chief Goose sighed. "OK, Joe, since Humpty's your brother,
I'll give you 'til five o'clock to play detective. If you don't
have anything by then, I'm writing that accident report."

I didn't have much time. I hurried to the hospital.
Thanks to the miracles of modern technology, combined
with some nifty techniques the doctors discovered when
Jack fell down and broke his crown, Humpty was on the
mend. But he didn't remember a thing. I needed to hit
the streets and question a few characters myself.

My first stop was the Bears'. I rang the doorbell three times and was about to give up when the door opened to reveal a bare foot. I was expecting a *bear* foot!

I showed the blonde my badge and asked about the Bears' whereabouts. "I'm house-sitting," she said, yawning.

"Late night?" I asked.

"Early morning. Some dog started howling and woke me up."

"How early?" I probed.

"Nine AM," she said. "But now that I'm awake, want to come in for some porridge?"

I hated to tell her no, but I was on the clock. And that clock was ticking.

Next house I visited belonged to the only dog owner in the neighborhood, Old Mother Hubbard. Maybe her pup had been howling this morning. But Mrs. H. said, "I gave my dog to the Farmer in the Dell last week. He needed help with his sheep, and unlike mine, his cupboard is never bare."

Mrs. H. shook her head sadly when I told her about Humpty. "I never would have done anything to Humpty, not even to feed my poor dog.

"Maybe you should talk to my neighbor," Mrs. H. added. "She seemed to be in a big hurry this morning."

Chicken Little answered the door looking more nervous than usual. "Am I in t-t-trouble?"

I played it cool. "You tell me," I said, keeping a close eye on her in case she tried to fly the coop.

"If it's about what happened this morning, it's not my fault," Chicken Little said.

"You know what happened this morning?"

"Of course I know!" she shouted. "The sky fell! And I didn't warn anyone. I've learned to keep my beak shut."

"The sky didn't fall this morning," I said. "Humpty did." From her surprised look, I knew she was innocent. "He's going to be OK," I said.

"I love that egg like he's one of my own," Chicken Little sniffled. I handed the tender chicken a tissue.

"So tell me where you were around nine," I said.

"I was on my morning power walk," she answered. "I'd just passed Muffy and Humpty when the wind howled overhead. I'd just walked behind the Wall, and the next thing I knew, the sky—I mean Humpty—was falling. I ran straight home."

"Was Humpty sitting on the Wall when you saw him?"

"Yes, but Muffy wasn't sitting on her tuffet." Chicken Little paused. "That's funny . . . she's usually digging into her curds and whey."

Funny indeed.

As I left my friend clucking to herself and scanning the sky, I heard a commotion coming from the Pigs' house—what was left of it, anyway.

Huff, puff, huff, puff. *I need more exercise*, I thought as I raced across the field. How many times had I heard people say that today? Not the "more exercise" part— the "huff, puff" part, as in "a huffy-puffy wind."

I found the Pigs fighting over, of all things, a cell phone. I thought everyone had one these days. Apparently not.

"OK, guys, hand it over," I said. "Whose phone is this?"

"We don't know," the pigs said. "We found it this morning after our house blew down."

Just then the phone rang. Actually, it howled.
Who would have a howl for a ring tone? I took a guess and disguised my voice. "Yo," I growled.

"I got the binoculars," the voice on the phone said.
"Now I want my yummy-wummy muffins. We had a deal, remember? Be at the Wall in five minutes."

I called Chief Goose and told her to meet me at the Wall.
The clues were adding up—the muffins that no one else
could buy, the howling that didn't come from a dog,
the huffy-puffy wind. Not to mention the binoculars that
someone wanted—bad! But why? I had a hunch.

Muffy was at the Wall, binoculars in hand. She didn't look too happy to see me. "Expecting someone else?" I asked. "Someone big and bad perhaps?"

"She's expecting me!" howled the Big Bad Wolf as he jumped out and grabbed the binoculars.

"Where are my muffins?" screamed Muffy. "I'm sick of curds and whey!"

"Sorry, doll, plan's changed," growled Wolf.

"You pushed Humpty off the Wall," I said. "I'm telling Chief Goose."

"I wasn't at the Wall this morning," Wolf said.

"But you *were* at the Pigs' house," I said, showing Wolf his phone. "When you blew down their house, you got Humpty, too. Guess you wanted a scrambled egg with your bacon."

"Wolf just wanted the binoculars," Muffy cried.
"He promised me some yummy-wummy muffins if I'd get them from Humpty. No one was supposed to get hurt!"

"And nobody else will, if you give me my phone, Joe, and get out of my way," Wolf snarled.

My, what big teeth he has, I thought. Where was Chief Goose?

"Hold it," shrieked Spider.

Talk about wrapping up a case!

"What's going on here?" Chief Goose had arrived.

"It seems that the howling wind this morning was actually Wolf blowing down the Pigs' new house—and Humpty along with it," I told the chief. "That's my theory, anyway."

"What about Muffy?" Chief asked.

"Actually, it's a conspiracy theory," I said. "Wolf promised our Little Miss muffins in exchange for Humpty's binoculars. Without the binoculars Humpty couldn't see Wolf blow down the Pigs' house."

"Apparently Wolf also threatened to blow down the Muffin Man's shop unless he got free muffins," Chief Goose said. "The guy's been hiding in a sack of sugar all day."

"Sweet," Wolf snarled.

Muffy glared at him. "I wouldn't have helped you if I'd known the truth. Humpty was my friend. Now he'll probably never speak to me again."

"You can always call him from your cell to apologize," I told her. "Your jail cell, that is."

"So, why'd you do it, Wolf?"
I asked.

"I'm Bad," he said,
shrugging his shoulders.
"It's my middle name."

"I have to hand it to you,
Joe," Chief Goose said, "you
were right. What happened to
Humpty really was a crime.
You weren't afraid to trust
your gut and get to the bottom
of this. I'm proud of you, Joe."

I have to admit, I was proud of me, too. And of my
brave friend Spider. In fact, Spider's the Neighborhood
Watch captain while Humpty's healing. As for me . . .

I've had plenty of cases to solve—dozens of 'em,
in fact. Word on the street is the Dish ran away with the
Spoon. And then there's my friend Bo. Bo Peep, that is.
That dame keeps me in business. Now, if I were a sheep,
where would I go?

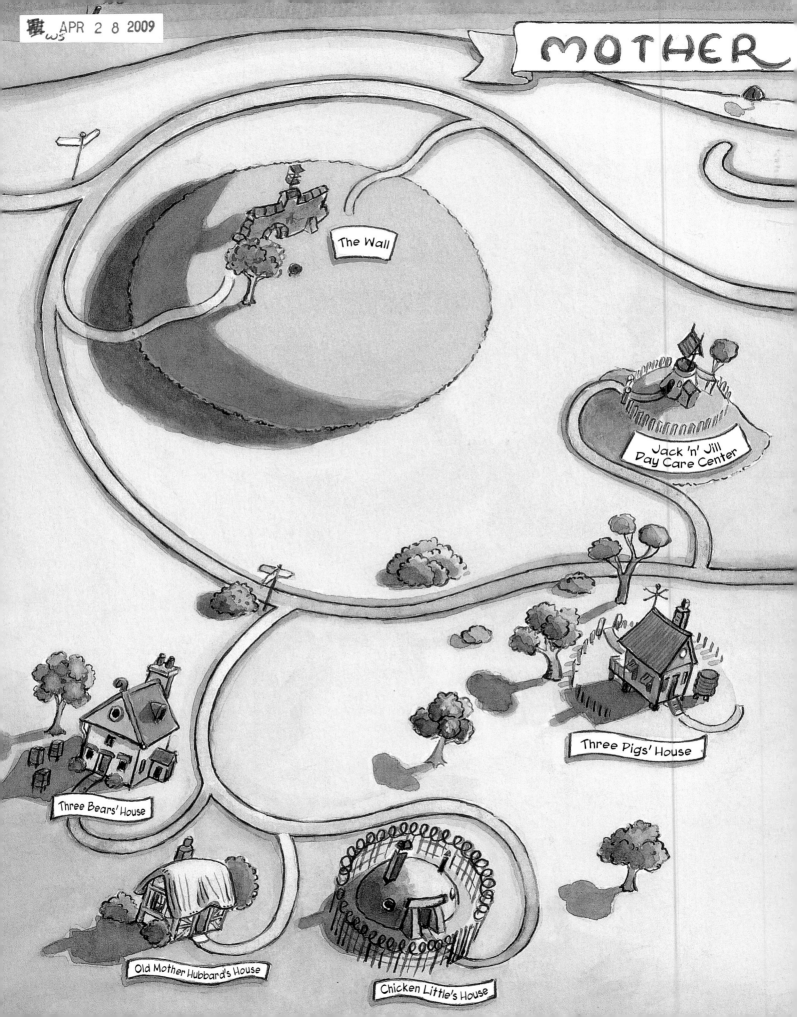

CAPTAIN TOMMY

Story by
Abby Ward Messner

Pictures by
Kim Harris Belliveau

Potential Unlimited Publishing FOUNDATION

Stratham, NH

**Potential Unlimited Publishing Foundation
would like to thank the following sponsors
for their generous financial support.**

international ltd.

*one tyco park
exeter, new hampshire
03833-1108*

**Wheelabrator
Technologies Inc.**

A WMX Technologies Company

WMX

Potential Unlimited Publishing
The PUP Foundation
P.O. Box 218
12 Evergreen Way
Stratham, NH 03885-0218
(603) 778-6006

Library of Congress Cataloging-in-Publication Data
Library of Congress Catalog Card Number: 96-92012
Main Entry Under Title: Captain Tommy
Story by Messner, Abby Ward
Illustrated by Belliveau, Kim Harris
Summary: A young boy at summer camp learns how to
befriend a peer who is challenged by autism.
1. Autism Spectrum Disorder — Juvenile Literature

First Edition
ISBN 0-9650700-0-X

To Richard, Richie and Laura—
the lights of my life.

-AWM

To my family for inspiration—
and friends for helping
make it happen.

-KHB

...

The art for each picture was created using
Berol Prismacolor Art Pencils
on Strathmore 60# Sketch Paper

My friend Kevin and I are going to Camp Acorn today.
We've never been to camp before. We're very excited!

My Mom checks to make sure we have our supplies...
sunscreen, sunglasses, bug spray, towels, bathing suits...
and then she checks again...and again!

"Come on, Mom! We're ready. Let's go!"

Mom is driving us to camp, and I made her promise not to kiss me in front of Kevin.

"'Bye Mom," I said, as we got out of the car.

"'Bye Mrs. Peacock," said Kevin.

"Good-bye Kevin—have fun! See you this afternoon, sweetheart," she says to me as she **blows** me a kiss. "Oh Mom!"

"Hey, Kevin, look at all the kids! And that big rock over there!
I bet I can beat you to the top!"

"No way!" Kevin said as he ran over to the rock.

When we got there, we saw a boy climbing the rock. Kevin and I both stopped and talked to him, but he kept climbing. When he got to the top, he slid down the other side. "Look, Kevin! We can slide down the rock too!"

Just then, the same boy came running around from behind the rock, jumped in our way and started to climb the rock again. "Hey! It's our turn!" I said, but he didn't even look at me. Up and over he went.

"Come on, Kevin. Let's go on the swings. We'll come back later."

The camp leader, Patty, called us inside. "Okay, everyone take a carpet square and have a seat around the circle."

Kevin and I sat next to each other. The boy we saw on the rock was sitting on my other side, rocking back and forth. A grown-up named Mrs. Walton was sitting behind us, whispering to him.

"Hello campers!" Patty said. It's nice to see your smiling faces!
I know some of you already, but let's go around the circle and tell
everyone your names."

The children said their names in turn. I said mine after Kevin.

When it was time for the boy next to me to say his name, he didn't say anything!

"Your turn," Patty said to him.

But the boy kept rocking and was now holding his hand in front of his face. He was watching his fingers wiggle. Mrs. Walton turned his head toward Patty and whispered, "Your turn, John."

"And what's your name?" Patty asked. There was no answer. Mrs. Walton whispered to the boy again.

"I John!" he yelled as he jumped up and ran around the room, flapping his arms like a bird. Mrs. Walton stood up and followed him as he headed for the door.

"What's he doing?" I whispered to Kevin. Kevin just looked out the door at him.

"As you know, this is spaceship week at Camp Acorn," said Patty. "All space people need equipment, so we'll be making space helmets this morning. But first, I would like you to play in groups of two so that you can get to know the other space travelers."

"Good!" I thought, thinking I could be with Kevin.

"Tommy!" I looked up, and there was Patty who asked me to follow her outside. Then she said, "I would like you to play with John."

"John? But I want to be with Kevin!" I pleaded.

"I know Kevin is your very good friend and that you enjoy doing things with him, but I could use your help in being with John."

I walked very slowly toward Mrs. Walton, who was watching John climb up the rock again. "What's the matter Tommy?" Mrs. Walton asked.

"I don't want to play with John. I don't think he likes me."

"What makes you say that Tommy?"

"Well, Kevin and I talked to him before and he didn't say anything. He didn't even look at us! Then he cut right in front of us when it was our turn! He's not very nice."

Mrs. Walton thought for a minute and said, "You know what, Tommy? You have a very special mission here at Camp Acorn today."

"What do you mean?" I asked.

"We're all pretending to be space people this week, right?" Mrs. Walton asked. "Pretend that you're the Captain of a big spaceship. One of the other ships isn't working properly and is floating out in space. As Captain, it's your job to help guide it back to the big ship, right?"

"How do I do that?" I asked, excited that she wanted me to be the Captain!

"Well, much like the ship that's lost in space, sometimes John feels lost when he's in a new place, with new people and new rules. Because of the different way John's brain works, John gets confused and uncomfortable sometimes and can't find the words to tell us how he is feeling. Doing things over and over again helps him feel better, like this morning when he kept climbing and sliding on the rock. I'm sure John didn't mean to hurt your feelings or be rude to you or Kevin. . .he was just trying not to feel so lost."

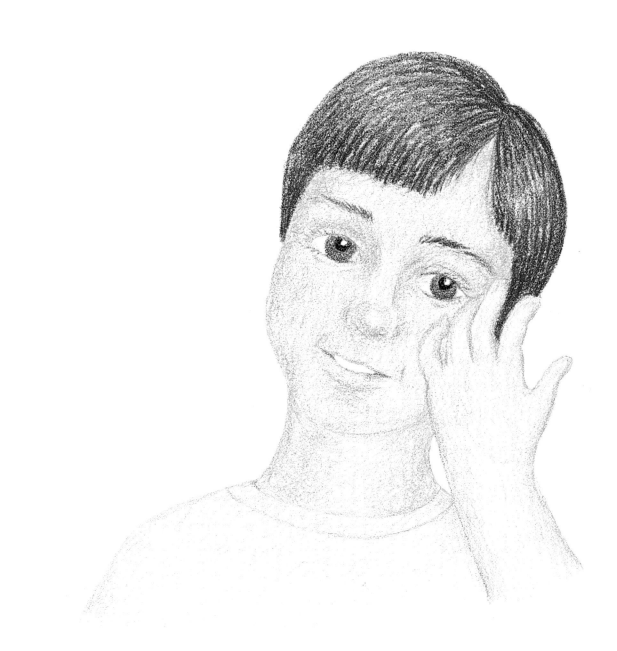

"Is that why he was rocking and wiggling his fingers in front of his eyes during circle?" Tommy asked.

"Exactly!" said Mrs. Walton. "Rocking and watching his fingers wiggle helps him to relax so he won't feel so uncomfortable."

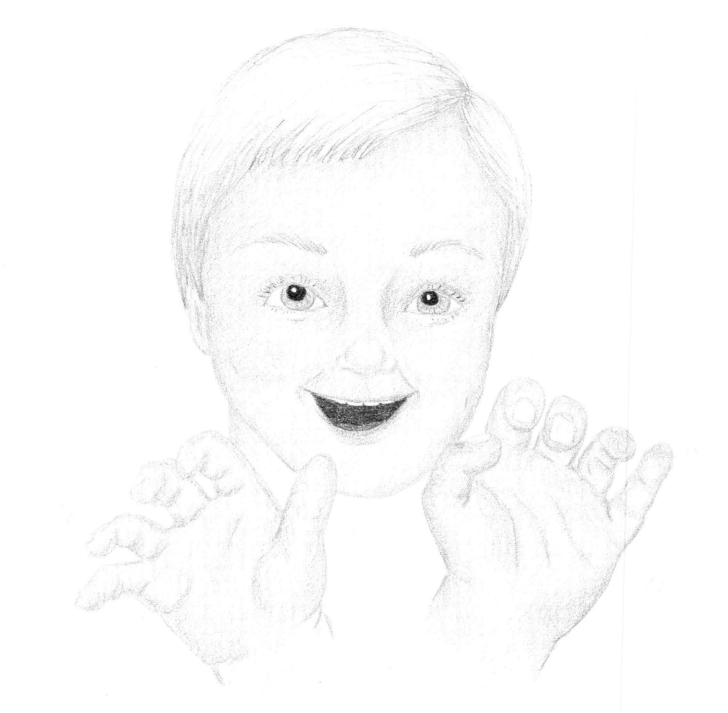

"Wow! Would it help if I wiggled my fingers in front of his eyes too?"

"Maybe, Tommy, but I think it would be even more helpful if you were to stand right in front of him, get him to look right at you, and talk to him very clearly. He might not answer right away, but as Captain of the ship, it's your job to think of ways to reach him."

"How about if I slide with him? Then I can show him where to go when we finish sliding."

"Perfect! A good Captain guides his ships where they need to go."

John and I took turns climbing and sliding on the rock. After a while he pointed at me and asked, "What's your name?"

"Tommy," I replied, really happy that he spoke first.
"What's yours?"

"I John."

"Hi John. Do you want to make space helmets with me?" I asked, pointing to the table where the other campers were busy cutting.
"Space people need space helmets."

John didn't say anything and started to climb up the rock again. "What do I do now, Mrs. Walton? He didn't answer me."

"Remember, a good Captain has to think of many different ways to bring in a lost ship. I think John needs you to say it in a different way."

Wanting to be a good captain, I climbed up the rock again. This time as I slid down I said, "Time to make our helmets!"

Then when John slid down again he said, "Time to make our helmets!"

John followed me over to the table where the other children were working. We each cut a hole in a big paper bag and glued a piece of blue see-through plastic over the hole. We added decorations to the outside, like flags and stars. Then we cut U-shaped pieces out of the sides of the bags so that our helmets could rest on our shoulders.

John had a hard time cutting with the scissors at first, so Mrs. Walton and I helped him a little.

"We did it, John! Now we're REAL space people!"

John put his helmet on, ran over to the jungle gym and quickly climbed to the very top. "I a spaceman!" he said proudly. Then he wrapped his legs around the fire pole and slid down.

"Wow! John, how did you do that? I can't even do that!" All the children watched John as he showed them how to slide down the "space pole."

"ALL SPACE PEOPLE, REPORT WITH YOUR HELMETS TO THE LAUNCH PAD!" ordered Patty.

"Come on, John, let's go!"

Patty told us to bend our knees as we started to count. . .

10 - 9 - 8 - 7 - 6 - 5 - 4 - 3 - 2 - 1 - 0 B L A S T - O F F !!!

We did it! And John counted backwards better and jumped higher than anybody!

"What a great job, boys!" Mrs. Walton said. Then she added, "And Tommy, you're a great Captain!"

I looked over at John and smiled. John was so excited he kept right on jumping!

Patty told us it was time to put our things away and to get ready to go. Kevin came over with both our backpacks. I was having such a good time with John that I almost forgot Kevin was there!

"Good-bye John," I said. "See you tomorrow!"

"Hi boys!" Mom said as we got into the car. "How was your first day at camp?"

"Great, Mom!" I replied. "We all got to be space people and Mrs. Walton said I was the Captain. I met a boy named John. His ship was lost in outer space and I helped him bring it back to the big ship. Then John taught us how to slide down the space pole and count down to blast-off!"

"My son, a spaceship Captain! Honey, I'm so proud of you."

"Oh Mom!"

ABOUT PUP BOOKS

Potential Unlimited Publishing (PUP) is a non-profit children's publishing company "dedicated to the belief that everyone needs friends."

PUP was founded in 1994 by three mothers of children with special needs attempting to facilitate the often difficult process through which their children are included in school, society and peer relationships. Toward PUP's goal of facilitating friendships, PUP's products are designed to encourage a heightened awareness of shared interests and talents, while providing a sensitive understanding of unique challenges. We at PUP believe that when common interests are found, real friendships can blossom.

For more information about PUP, or to order additional copies of <u>Captain Tommy</u>, please contact:

Potential Unlimited Publishing
P.O. Box 218
Stratham, NH 03885-0218
(603) 778-6006

The author and illustrator would like to express their appreciation to the following people who have lent their energy and many talents toward the completion of <u>Captain Tommy</u>:

PUP's Staff
Karen Powers, Janet Alperin, Nicole Bock and Claire Anderson

PUP's Board of Directors
Miriam Stahl, Donna Wilson, Linda Tailleart, Jean Waldron, Raymond Dostie
Marjorie Dostie, Roger Anderson and Marian Reilly

PUP's Consultants and Friends
Richard Messner, Ph.D., Assoc. Professor, University of New Hampshire
Julie Griffin, C.Ht., Author/Publisher, Griffin-Meads Products, Everett, MA
Mary Bamford, OTR, Occupational Therapist, Stratham Memorial School
Thomas McCormack, MSW, Therapist, Mill Pond Mental Health, Portsmouth, NH
Sharon Griffin, M.A., CCC/SLP, Speech Pathologist, Exeter Hospital, Exeter, NH
Felicia Donovan, Technology Coordinator, Stratham Memorial School
Carrie Torney, Author/Publisher, Friends of Nick, Claremont, NH
Richard Wainwright, Author/Publisher, Family Life Publishing, Dennis, MA

PUP would also like to thank Jean Waldron and The Acorn School of Stratham, NH for inspiring this remarkable fact-based story.